Mrs. Biddlebox

By Linda Smith

Illustrated by Marla Frazee

HarperCollinsPublishers

To my agent and wonderful friend,

Steve Malk, who believed in me,

my editor, Alix Reid,

and my husband, Russ.

L. S.

To Andrea, my bud.

M. F.

Mrs. Biddlebox• Text copyright © 2002 by Linda Smith • Illustrations copyright © 2002 by Marla Frazee • Printed in Hong Kong. All rights reserved.
www.harperchildrens.com • Library of Congress Cataloging-in-Publication Data • Smith, Linda, date • Mrs. Biddlebox / by Linda Smith ; illustrated by Marla Frazee.
p.   cm. • Summary: With baking magic, Mrs. Biddlebox uses fog, dirt, sky, and other ingredients of a rotten day to transform it into a sweet cake.
ISBN 0-06-028690-3 — ISBN 0-06-029782-4 (lib. bdg.) • [1. Emotions—Fiction. 2. Cake—Fiction. 3. Baking—Fiction. 4. Stories in rhyme.] I. Frazee, Marla, ill.
II. Title. • PZ8.3.3S6542 Mr 2002 • 00-063199 • [E]—dc21 • CIP AC • Typography by Stephanie Bart-Horvath 1 2 3 4 5 6 7 8 9 10 ❖ First Edition

On a knotty little hill,
In a dreary little funk,
Mrs. Biddlebox rolled over
On the wrong side of her bunk.

The birds gave her a headache.
There were creakies in her chair.
A breeze blew dank and dreary
And mussied up her hair.

So she slammed the door on morning!
And sat thinking what to do.
Her tea was dark and bitter,
Her crumpets hard to chew.

With her belly full of grumblies
And her hands upon her hips,
An idea burst inside her
And whizzled from her lips!

I will cook this rotten morning!
I will turn it into cake!
I will fire up my oven!
I will set the day to bake!

Mrs. Biddlebox got busy.
She grabbed a pot and broom.
She tromped out into morning
To gather up the gloom.

She snatched a patch of grubby lawn.
She scuffled with the dirt.

She plucked a filthy shadow
From the folds of her old skirt.

When the fog gave her the whiffles,
She held her broomstick steady,
Stabbed the dreary lot of it,
And twirled it like spaghetti!

Mrs. Biddlebox reached up
And hooked a ray of sun,
Then yanked it like a ball of yarn
Until it came undone.

She rolled the sky like carpeting
(The birdies flew away).

Now the pot was overflowing
with that DESPICABLE bad day.

So she whipped and whisked and beat it.
She rolled the day out flat.
Mrs. Biddlebox laughed gleefully;
Her hands went *pat-pat-pat*.

When the dough was finally finished,
When it rose up fat and light,
She stomped it down into a tin
With witchety delight!

And oh! The day baked merrily!
And oh! The spicy heat!

Mrs. Biddlebox could not deny
It was turning out quite sweet!

She poured a cup of lovely tea.
She set a pretty plate.
She cut a merry slice of cake
And ate . . .

and ATE . . .

and ATE!

Now with her belly full of crumblies
And her nighty cap pulled tight,
She threw the door wide open
And welcomed in the night!

On a knotty little hill,
In a cozy little heap,
Mrs. Biddlebox rolled over,
Closed her eyes,

And went to sleep.